RACE THE WILD

ARCTIC FREEZE

RACE THE WILD

ARE YOU READY TO RUN THE WILDEST RACE OF YOUR LIFE?

Course #1: Rain Forest Relay

Course #2: Great Reef Games

Course #3: Arctic Freeze

RACE THE WILD

ARCTIC FREEZE

·BY **KRISTIN EARHART**·
·ILLUSTRATED BY **EDA KABAN**·

SCHOLASTIC INC.

Text copyright © 2015 by Kristin Earhart
Illustrations copyright © 2015 by Scholastic Inc.

All rights reserved. Published by Scholastic Inc., *Publishers since 1920*. SCHOLASTIC and associated logos are trademarks and/or registered trademarks of Scholastic Inc.

The publisher does not have any control over and does not assume any responsibility for author or third-party websites or their content.

No part of this publication may be reproduced, stored in a retrieval system, or transmitted in any form or by any means, electronic, mechanical, photocopying, recording, or otherwise, without written permission of the publisher. For information regarding permission, write to Scholastic Inc., Attention: Permissions Department, 557 Broadway, New York, NY 10012.

This book is a work of fiction. Names, characters, places, and incidents are either the product of the author's imagination or are used fictitiously, and any resemblance to actual persons, living or dead, business establishments, events, or locales is entirely coincidental.

ISBN 978-0-545-77355-3

10 9 8 7 6   16 17 18 19

Printed in the U.S.A.   40
First printing 2015

Book design by Yaffa Jaskoll

TO CHLOE, WHO IS A DREAM
READER —KJE

CHAPTER 1

SHORTS IN THE SNOW

In the summer sun, the snow was a fierce white. Dev squinted, trying to make out the trail. The dogs forged ahead, and the slice of the sled's runners on the ice filled Dev's ears. He glanced over his shoulder at the other sleds. His teammates were only a few lengths behind him.

Working together, the dogs pulled Dev's sled almost effortlessly. Dev focused on the lead dog, on his right. She was a reliable husky, mostly white with a pale caramel-colored frosting on her head and back. *Tucker.* He said her name to himself. He trusted her to be steady and find the path.

Out of the corner of his eye, he spotted a bald eagle. The bird rode an air current, soaring in the blue sky without a single flap of its wings. Dev took a deep breath. The cold air stunned his nostrils.

This scene was everything he had imagined when he sent in his application for *The Wild Life*, a once-in-a-lifetime chance to trek through extreme habitats, gathering animal facts in hopes of winning the entire race . . . and a million dollars.

Of course, that money would be split between the four members of the team, but Dev didn't have a problem with that. He wasn't in it for the money. He just wanted the chance to do something new, something different, something challenging. Now, he was driving a team of huskies through the frosty wilderness in northern Alaska, heading toward the Arctic Circle. He was certain he had made the right choice.

On one side of the sled he saw a lanky moose with mighty antlers, on the other a polar bear, floating on a chunk of Arctic ice. Then his eyes focused in on something directly ahead, right in the dogs' path. It looked like a man—a man wearing plaid shorts and sandals. The dogs did not slow down, and the person did not move. Only when the lead dog was nearly on top of the man did Dev realize it was his dad . . .

A splash of water tickled Dev's face and swept his thoughts back to the waking world. Even though he had woken up hours ago, he couldn't shake the dream. It had been the most vivid of his life, and now it was haunting him. It had seemed so real, right down to his dad's outfit. But why was his dad, who planned for absolutely everything, wearing shorts in the snow? Dev suspected it had something to do with the way he'd left things with his father before the race began. If it had been up to his dad, Dev would be wearing shorts right now, sitting in front of a computer at science camp.

Maybe that was why the dream was taking over his thoughts when there were far better things to think about, like the race. *The Wild Life* was not a dream. He was competing in it! He was on the third leg! And he was in the middle of a chilly, rushing Alaskan stream!

"Are we there yet?" he called out, trying to regain his focus. He had not known his three teammates before the start of the race, but they had all earned his trust. The four members of Team Red—Sage, Russell, Mari, and Dev—had learned a lot in the race's first two legs. After challenging courses in the Amazon rain forest and the Great Barrier Reef, they were currently in second place. At least they had been in second at the start of the day when the teams all began the trek into the Arctic.

"We'll get there when we find what we're looking for." That was Sage, the self-appointed leader of Team Red. Her straight strawberry-blonde hair swung with each sure-footed stride. She didn't need to turn around for Dev to feel the intensity of her steely gaze. It was a good thing Sage took charge, because no one else wanted that responsibility. Not even Dev. Especially not

Dev. "You do remember that you're the one with the GPS, don't you?"

That was true. When they were selecting supplies, Dev always went for the gadgets. For this leg of the race, he chose the fancy GPS so he could help plan their routes. Alaska was a big place. They didn't have time to get lost.

Dev glanced around, taking in the lush green of the leaves. There were key differences from his dream. It was summer, which meant that the snow had melted. They were near the coast in southern Alaska. Instead of dogsleds, they were on foot. And right now, both his feet were dry inside a pair of waist-high waders—the waterproof overalls that fishermen usually wear. The waders were way cooler than plaid shorts. That was for sure.

"Mari, where are we going to find a grizzly bear?" Dev asked. He knew Mari would be nice, and there was a chance she could actually answer the question. Mari had a sixth sense for animals. She knew almost everything about them, which really came in handy on a race that was all about animals and ecosystems.

"Well, going by what you showed us on the GPS, this stream connects with a river," Mari replied. Unlike Sage, she did turn around, her warm brown eyes locking with Dev's. With all the sun, her tan skin had deepened to a rich caramel since the first leg of the race. "It should be on the other side of this bank. There's a good chance salmon will be swimming upstream in that river, and grizzlies will be waiting for them."

That was right. Dev remembered now. Their first challenge had been to track down a grizzly bear, but grizzlies could be unpredictable. Mari had recommended staying as far away from them as possible. The team's chaperone, Javier, had said that was a good idea. Even though Javier was not allowed to give the team hints, he was as cool as a guide could get. He would sometimes offer advice, especially in dangerous situations.

Everyone agreed it might be easiest—and safest—to find a bear where there was a reliable food source. That way, the bear would be focused on the food, so the kids could take a picture and move on as quickly as possible.

Taking the picture would be up to Dev. He was in charge of the ancam, which was kind of like a walkie-talkie and a camera all in one. The race organizers sent the teams clues over the ancam, and then the teams sent the answers back. Usually, the answers were in the form of photos. That's what they had to do now. Once they sent in a picture of a grizzly, they would get the next clue. Dev patted the team's trusty ancam. He had it safely stashed in the inside pocket of his jacket.

"We may see lots of grizzlies," Mari added. "They know that the salmon are starting to swim upstream this time of year, returning to the place where they were born so they can spawn."

"I know what spawning means in a video game," Russell called from the bank of the stream. "But I don't think the salmon are coming back to life after being killed by an acid-breathing dragon."

"Not exactly," Mari said without even cracking a smile. "Spawning is when fish lay and fertilize eggs, so new fish can be born. Salmon do it in the exact same place where they hatched years before. Some swim thousands of miles to get there."

Dev admired Mari. She had all this knowledge, but she was super humble about it.

"So, if Dev is right, the river will be on the other side of that hill," Sage announced. "We're climbing up to see if there are any bears." She, Russell, and Javier quickly disappeared over the grassy bank while Mari and Dev made their way to the edge of the stream.

Dev was starting to feel like his head was back in the race. He thought ahead to what angle might be good for the grizzly photo. The sun was strong.

He'd have to be careful that it didn't mess up the light in the picture. Sometimes there was only enough time for one good shot.

With his mind on the photo, he didn't notice that the floor of the stream bed was getting mucky as they neared the shore. Mari must not have noticed either. The water was above his knees when he realized he was stuck.

"Um, I can't move," Mari announced from behind him.

"I can't either," Dev said, his tone even.

"I mean it," Mari said. Her pitch was rising high above the rush of the brisk water.

"I know, but you have to stay calm," Dev said. "I think we're stuck in some kind of quicksand. If you struggle, you could sink deeper." Dev's words came out slow and steady, but his mind was in a frenzied whirl—trying to solve the problem like a puzzle, trying to do what he did best.

THE ARCTIC

The Arctic is the region at the northernmost part of Earth. It is marked by an imaginary line that circles the top of the planet. The Antarctic is on the other side, on the southernmost part of the planet. The points at the very top and bottom are called the North Pole and the South Pole.

The Arctic region includes the northern parts of Greenland, Russia, Scandinavia, Canada, and Alaska, which is one of the United States. Despite the especially long and cold winters, people still live in these regions. Many are native to the Arctic, including the Inuit, Sami (sometimes called Laplanders), Greenlanders, and Yakuts.

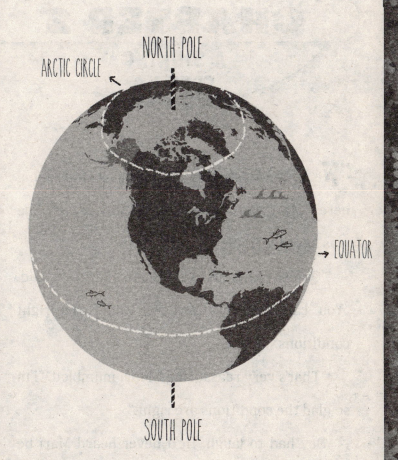

NORTH POLE

ARCTIC CIRCLE

EQUATOR

SOUTH POLE

CHAPTER 2

A SINKING FEELING

"**W**e're in Alaska! What is quicksand doing here?" Mari was not taking Dev's advice well. She was anything but calm.

"Quicksand is just very wet sand," Dev said. "You can find it anywhere, under the right conditions."

"That's very reassuring," Mari mumbled. "I'm so glad the conditions are right."

Dev had to laugh. He'd never heard Mari be sarcastic before.

"We'll be fine. We're not in that deep. We just need a little help," he tried to reassure her. "Guys! Come back! Guys!"

Nothing. Dev's calls seemed to be swallowed by the sound of the stream. The rest of the team was upwind, on the other side of the bank. The moving air would carry the sound waves in the opposite direction. Their teammates would never hear him.

"Okay, Mari," he began. He tried to think through what quicksand was and how it worked. "Here's what we have to do. Quicksand is denser than we are, so we can float on it. We just have to tilt forward, and let the quicksand hold us up."

"Are you crazy?" Mari said under her breath. She stared at the quicksand as if it were alive, like a clawed fist would reach out at any moment and pull her down. She took a deep breath and screamed, "Help! Help! You guys!"

"I'm not crazy." Dev tried to sound as sane as possible. "Think about it. You can float on water. This quicksand is way more dense than that. It's thicker! It can hold us." Dev couldn't even remember where he had read it, but he knew that quicksand was just sand that had more water around it. The water made the sand slippery, so the grains didn't stick together to make a more solid surface. It was hard to explain. Dev realized he probably *did* sound crazy. Science didn't make much sense when it felt like the ground was sucking you down, but they had not sunk any deeper. That was reassuring.

Dev dropped his backpack to shed weight. Then he pitched his body forward. He could feel the muck spread under his chest as his feet lifted from the floor of the riverbed.

"Stay there," he advised Mari. "Don't move. I'll get you out."

Mari didn't say anything, but watched Dev as he searched for some leverage in the spongy dirt. With bent knees, he began to monkey crawl across the muddy sand. His chin grazed the muck with each push of his knees and elbows. He tried to make himself as flat as possible, to spread out over the surface so he wouldn't sink.

A sharp, ripe aroma rose from the wet earth. The cold goo oozed all around Dev. He pushed himself farther and finally fumbled onto solid ground. Then he rolled over and filled his lungs with air. As he breathed in, he looked back at

Mari. He was less than ten feet from her, but it felt like miles.

"What's going on?" a voice called from above.

"Sage! Help!" Mari called.

Dev forced himself up to sit. "We're stuck! It's quicksand!"

Sage, Russell, and Javier scrambled down the hill, their faces confused and scared.

"Quick, Russell, grab that branch!" Javier directed. Russell lifted a long, gnarled stick from the edge of the bank. He held one end out to their guide.

"I think we came up the bank about there," Sage said, pointing. "Maybe it's safer?"

Russell and Javier judged the footing and stepped carefully. Javier held out the branch as far as he could.

Mari grabbed it with stiff red hands. The mud slurped as she braced herself and tried to tug her legs from the thick muck. "No good," she said.

"Undo your waders," Javier directed.

"What?" Mari asked.

"You have long underwear on, right?"

Mari nodded.

"If you unlatch your waders and wiggle your legs a little, I think we'll be able to get you out."

Javier dragged a log from the bank. He stretched himself across it. As soon as Mari had unbuckled her waterproof overalls, she reached out to him. She wriggled around and pulled her legs out, one at a time. Javier guided her as she lurched on her knees through the shallow mud, landing on solid ground next to Dev. Her thick dark braid was crusted with mud.

"Sorry. I couldn't do it like you," she said to Dev.

"Doesn't matter." When he slapped his hand against her backpack, he couldn't help but think how lucky she was. The bag's extra weight could have pulled her down.

"That was a close call," Javier said, dragging his hand across his forehead. "I hadn't thought we'd have a problem this far inland. Quicksand can be much worse."

"My bag's still in there," Dev said, motioning. The hiking pack was halfway submerged in the sand.

Javier shook his head. "Leave it," he said, leaning on the branch. "No way am I letting anyone get close to it. Maybe the race organizers will retrieve it for you. I can request dry clothes at the next pit stop."

"How'd you get out?" Russell asked.

Dev shrugged. Normally, he would have made a joke about not being "in too deep," but he held himself back. He was too shaken to joke around, and for Dev, that was saying something.

"Do you have the ancam?" Sage questioned. Her voice was apologetic.

"Yep," Dev said, patting his chest pocket.

Sage looked relieved. Dev got it. She was concerned about her teammates, but she also was practical. They were still running a race, after all.

CREATURE FEATURE

BROWN BEAR

SCIENTIFIC NAME: *Ursus arctos*

TYPE: mammal

RANGE: widely spread across northern sections of North America, Europe, and Asia

FOOD: berries; nuts; fruit; roots; fish, especially salmon; and mammals, from rodents to moose

"Grizzly bear" is a type of brown bear. This name is only used in North America. It refers to the same subspecies of brown bear found in Russia, Europe, and Asia.

Brown bears have long snouts and small rounded ears. They have a pronounced hump on their shoulders, which is actually extra, bulky muscle to make them good diggers. With their strong shoulders and extra-long claws, brown bears dig up plenty of roots for dinner, and underground dens for hibernating through the frigid winter months.

Brown bears are typically brown (no surprise there), but grizzly bears have thick fur that is often white at its tips. This is how they got their nickname, since "grizzled" means "graying."

CHAPTER 3

UPSTREAM BATTLE

"**A**re you sure you guys are okay?" Javier asked, looking from Dev to Mari.

"I'm sure," Dev insisted.

"Yeah," said Mari. She gulped from her canteen.

Russell handed Dev his water bottle. "Here, man." As he took it, Dev realized that Russell's smile was not as wide as usual, his kind eyes more serious.

"When you guys are up to it, there's a whole posse of grizzlies just over the bank," Sage informed them. That was good news. Dev needed a plan. He did not need anything else to distract him from the race.

Mari borrowed an extra pair of waders from Sage. They were two sizes too big, but she used a bungee cord as a makeshift belt. She knotted it tight and started up the incline with the others.

"Take me to the grizzlies," Dev said. "I can't *bear* the suspense!"

"I can't bear your bad jokes," Russell mumbled. He gave Dev a sturdy knock with his elbow.

But when they reached the top of the hill, they were all speechless. There was a steep, rugged drop on the other side. The river was wide, bordered by lush green trees and grasses that jutted out between ancient gray boulders. The waterway took turns, meandering around high banks and the rocky shore. Not very far upstream was a crystal-clear waterfall that stretched the full width of the river.

Perched on the higher level of the waterfall were four grizzly bears. Another three stood on the lower level, chest-deep. The two groups faced each other, surveying the crashing water between them.

"I thought grizzlies were solitary," Sage whispered.

"They are. Except for moms and cubs, they usually live alone," Mari confirmed. "But they put up with other bears this time of year. They all want in on the food fest."

That's when Dev saw the fish. Where the water cascaded downward, silver fish arced into the air, battling the plunging current. The fish were salmon, and everywhere Dev saw one, there was also a giant brown bear. The bears stood with their heads tilted to the side. As soon as a fish blasted out of the water, a bear's mighty jaws snapped on it.

"They're just leaping into the bears' mouths," Sage said.

"It looks like that," Javier responded, "but scientists say that for every fish that is caught, one hundred get by."

"The bears have a surefire strategy," Russell said. "It's impressive."

"I think the salmon are impressive," Mari said. "They put all they've got into this trip. Their

bodies change so that they can function in the river's fresh water after being in salt water their entire adult lives. It's pretty crazy."

"How do they know where to go?" Russell asked.

"It's kind of a mystery," Mari said. "Scientists think it might be their sense of smell."

Dev tried to wrap his head around that: the fact that the fish trusted their instincts to lead them back to where they had been born. That wasn't the way Dev thought at all. He'd want proof, a landmark or something. No way would he just smell his way somewhere.

On top of everything else, Dev knew Mari was leaving out one key fact. The salmon died after they spawned. This journey would be their last.

"Okay, I'll admit, I could watch this all day, but let's not forget why we're here." Leave it to Sage to get them back on track.

Dev had been so captivated that he had almost forgotten to snap the photo. He slipped out the ancam and focused in on one of the mighty bears. With the trees blocking some of the sunlight, he was able to get a good shot. "Got it," he said as he sent the image to Bull Gordon, the rugged spokesperson for *The Wild Life*. He was certain Bull would approve it.

The teams had only seen the world-class adventurer at the start and finish of each leg, but Bull Gordon's big personality seemed to cheer them through each challenge. At no point did Bull suggest that the race was a battle of man versus nature. He insisted people had a responsibility to respect and protect the wild world. The more Dev learned, the more he felt the same.

Almost immediately, he felt the familiar buzz of the ancam. "We've got our next clue!" he announced. He read aloud.

```
        No little dears,
  New in spring, deadly in fall,
    Branching like leaves,
   On the largest of all.
```

"Now that's not bad," Dev said when he had finished. All throughout the race, he had cringed at the forced poetry of the clues. Dev liked a good pun, but he hated a bad rhyme.

"I'm glad you think the clue deserves extra credit for creative merit, but do you have any idea what it means?" Sage questioned. The skin between her eyebrows creased into a deep V as she read the clue again. They all looked to Mari.

"We can figure this out," Mari answered. "I know *little dear* isn't spelled like the animal, but it's an obvious hint."

"I'm pretty sure *largest of them all* is, too," Dev added. "The largest deer is the moose, but they don't just want a picture of a moose."

"They want the antlers," Russell realized. "Only the male moose have them. They grow new ones in the spring and then fight with them in the fall. The bigger the better."

"Nice work, guys," Sage said with a smile, and the V instantly disappeared. "So where do we find a set of those big antlers?"

"Attached to a big moose," Dev answered.

CREATURE FEATURE

MOOSE

SCIENTIFIC NAME: *Alces alces*

TYPE: mammal

RANGE: widely spread across northern sections of North America and Asia

FOOD: aquatic plants like grasses and lily pads, twigs, bark, even pinecones

Besides being the largest deer, the moose is the only deer that can feed in the water. Equipped with nostrils that can seal shut, moose wade into streams and rivers to eat aquatic plants. They can even dive underwater to escape a wolf—or nasty, nippy bugs—for up to 30 seconds.

With its long, skinny legs, droopy muzzle, and floppy throat flap, the moose might look like a mess of odd features, but its body is fully functional. Those legs help it run exceptionally well—up to thirty-five miles per hour. A calf can outrun a human when it's just five days old! Its nose gives the moose a super sense of smell. And the flap of skin hanging from its throat is called a bell. Scientists are not sure what it does yet!

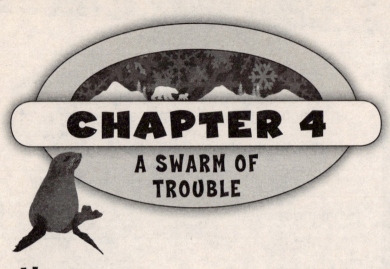

CHAPTER 4

A SWARM OF TROUBLE

With the way Dev's brain worked, he sometimes couldn't stop himself from making a bad joke. But he took a lot of things seriously, which was part of the reason he was in charge of the GPS. The other part was that he loved gadgets. At home, he took apart old phones and radios just for fun.

His grandparents had given him a book called *The Way Things Work* when he was six. He had secretly read it after bedtime and slept with it under his pillow for weeks before his mom found out. She'd laughed as she shook her head. "You're just like your father," she'd said.

Because he had the GPS, it was Dev's job to help the red team find the fastest—and safest—route to the moose's roaming grounds.

"Do we really have to stick to this trail?" Sage asked, easing her way along the thin path. A steep cliff rose on one side, and a ridge dropped on the other. "We aren't looking for a mountain goat."

"Yeah, I thought moose were more common on the forest floor," Russell added.

"That's true," Mari said.

"We need to wait until a marked path branches off downhill," Dev said. "Or else we could set off a rock slide." Dev made it sound casual, but he had thought it through. In this part of Alaska, snow might cling to the ground until April or May, when it would finally melt. Dev knew that the extra water had to go somewhere. Plus, there'd been a downpour the night before. That much wetness would make the ground unstable, which meant rockslides. Dev had already seen several piles of rubble at the bottom of the ridge.

He scanned the horizon. What a view: blue skies, the deep green peaks of endless evergreen trees, crystal-white mountaintops in the distance. You couldn't see anything like this in a computer lab. Looking out over the expanse almost made Dev forget that world even existed.

"There's a lake over that way," he pointed out. "A good path has to head down to it soon. That's our best bet."

They walked for forty minutes and passed a few rocky trails heading down the mountain that

Dev quickly nixed as too dangerous. Finally they found one that looked clear, and took it. Dev was sure they'd lost time, but he was also certain it was smart to play it safe.

"At last. Thank goodness," Sage said, wiping the sweat from her forehead. The temperature was pleasantly mild for summer—comfortable for hiking in long sleeves and cargo pants—but the sun was strong and they were moving fast.

The new path eased downward with brush and bushes growing on either side. As they descended, the air grew still. Evergreen branches arched over them, a natural shelter from the sun. But they didn't keep the bugs out.

"Where did these mosquitos come from?" Russell asked, using both hands to shoo the pests from his face.

"Technically?" Dev asked. "They came from eggs. Then larva. Then pupae."

"Um, I wasn't asking for a report on the life cycle of the mosquito," Russell said.

Dev had meant it to be funny, but nothing seemed very funny when under attack by a swarm of blood-thirsty insects. Dev's arms were growing tired of swatting.

"They're worse down here because there's no wind," Dev tried again. "And we're getting closer to water."

"I feel like there's a big sign above my head that reads, 'Hey, mosquitos! All you can eat buffet! Come and get it!' " Russell complained.

"There are at least thirty-five different species of mosquitos in Alaska," Javier said from the back of the line. "They're part of the reason we

suggested you dress in layers. The less skin exposed, the better."

"Some people call them the state bird of Alaska," Mari commented. "Because they get so big here." Dev frowned. It was a silly saying. Mosquitos weren't anything like birds. They were insects: cold-blooded, six-legged beasts. Not all insects even had wings. Plus, there was the whole not having feathers thing.

Right now, Dev felt the "cold-blooded" part was especially true of the mosquitos. They showed no mercy!

"These things are big enough to show up on satellite," Russell huffed.

"They aren't nearly as big as that guy," Sage announced, suddenly whispering.

The group stumbled to a stop, huddled right behind Sage. They had come to the edge of a wide streambed. On the other side, a moose was easing its way into the slow-moving water. Its long, skinny legs looked like toothpicks under its large, hairy brick of a body.

Dev unzipped his jacket and slid out the ancam. Leaning forward, he snapped a shot with the moose's large antlers at the center. Unlike those of a deer, the moose's antlers had the shape of a leaf with many sharp prongs poking out.

"Gorgeous," he murmured. Out of the corner of his eye, he saw Russell smirk.

"Did you get it?" Sage asked. "Are you sure the picture isn't of a cloud of mosquitos?"

"I'm sure," Dev said with a smile. Sage had always been one to ask pointed questions, but she had recently developed a sense of humor about it. "And I have the next clue to prove it," Dev added, studying the ancam screen. "It's a map with a red pin. The place marked is on the lake we saw from the trail above. Let's go."

CREATURE FEATURE

MOSQUITO

SCIENTIFIC NAME: *Culicidae*

TYPE: insect

RANGE: worldwide

FOOD: females—blood; males—nectar

Mosquitos have four life stages: egg, larva, pupa, and adult. All stages live in water except the adult. Female mosquitos lay their eggs in late summer. In most species, the eggs live through the winter and do not begin growing into the next stage until the water warms up in late spring.

Because there is a lot of standing and slow-moving water in Alaska after the snow melts, it's a prime habitat for mosquitos.

Only female mosquitos feed on blood. Each female has a needle-like mouthpart that pierces human and animal skin and injects saliva. The saliva contains a chemical that keeps the blood from clotting.

Why does skin puff up and get itchy? It's usually from an allergic reaction to the insect's saliva.

CHAPTER 5

TEAM RED TAKES A HIKE

"**S**eriously?" Sage stared into the sky. The others shielded their eyes from the sun as they looked to the far end of the lake. They had followed Dev's every direction to the highlighted location, but all they found was the dwindling exhaust of a small plane. It was only a couple hundred feet above the lake's surface, and had to have just taken off. "This is right where the clue led us. How did someone beat us here?"

It was a rhetorical question. Sage didn't expect anyone to answer, but Dev had to stop himself from commenting. There was only one explanation: He'd taken them the long way around the ridge to avoid rockslides, and it had cost them time. It was his fault they'd been left choking on the plane's fumes.

"Wait. There's a new pin on the map," Dev informed Team Red. "It's just north of here, right on the lake."

"We have to hike farther?" Mari asked. "That hardly seems fair."

"At least the mosquitos aren't as bad in the sun," Javier said, trying to sound upbeat. Dev appreciated that.

"Should we be keeping quiet?" Sage wondered.

"What if we scare off all the animals? We never know when a new clue is going to just pop up on the ancam."

"I wouldn't worry about that," Javier reassured them. "It's best to let the animals know you're here, grizzlies especially. You don't want to catch them off guard. After all, this is their home, their territory. We have to respect that."

Instead of talking like Javier had suggested, everyone fell silent, thinking about this wild place and all the animals that lived with its extreme weather—sunny and warm with plentiful food in the summer; harsh and cold, bitter and bare in the winter.

"It's getting kind of late, isn't it?" Sage asked after a while. "Maybe we should try to speed up.

What if we have to get a shot from the plane? It'd be hard in the dark."

That was just like Sage, always thinking. But Dev was one step ahead of her. "It won't get dark for a long time," Dev said. "We're in Alaska, Land of the Midnight Sun. Because of the tilt of Earth, the days are especially long near the North Pole in the summer. And they're especially short in the winter. If we can get to that next plane first, we'll be fine."

The whole team went silent again. Dev's hiking boots felt heavy on his feet, but he was thankful for them. The bank of the lake was marshy and scattered with rocks. For stretches, the pine trees grew right up to the water, forcing the team to climb around the long slick needles and pinecones that littered the embankment. And like almost everywhere they'd looked since they landed in Alaska, up ahead were mountains, frosted on top with everlasting snow.

"There it is!" Sage cried as they emerged from a cluster of trees.

On cue, they all started running.

The plane was pulled up to a short dock. Instead of wheels, it had what looked like large torpedoes that rested on the water. Of course, they weren't torpedoes. They were pontoons, full of air and buoyant enough to keep the whole plane afloat. Dev had always been amazed that a plane could take off on water, using almost the exact same physics that it did on land. The plane just needed the pontoons, and its propeller, wings, and flaps would get it in the air the exact same way.

The team scrambled into the back of the plane

as Javier introduced himself to the pilot, who wore a baseball hat and a fishing vest.

"We have the next clue," Dev said after checking the ancam. "It's long." Dev began to read, trying to project over the rhythmic whir of the propeller charging up.

From water to sky
On this landmass
None is as high.
From there, head west
To track down a pack
That is tracking down a herd
In which all wear a rack.

To finish the clue, you must
submit three photos.

Dev still didn't get why the clues had to rhyme. At least it made sense. Dev was pretty sure he knew two of the answers. "The first one has to be Mount McKinley," he announced. "It's the highest peak on the continent." The rest of the team nodded. "And we all know which animal is famous for hunting in a pack." They nodded again. "What about the last one?"

"Well, 'rack' is another term for antlers, right?" Mari began. She glanced around the cramped cabin. "And female caribou have antlers, as well as males. Caribou are the only deer like that. I think that's what they mean by 'all.' Of course, the young reindeer don't have them, so you can't say it's a real fact."

"And you can't say that the clue is real poetry, but I guess it's close enough." Dev started punching buttons on the GPS. "Just a second," he murmured. "Double-checking the coordinates." After some more button pushing, he had directions to give the pilot. Dev was determined that they would make up the time they'd lost.

Dev watched out the window as the plane teetered off the lake. He had never been in a small plane before. The engine was noisy, and the sky was all around. As the plane gained height, Dev thought about how the plane defied the pull of gravity toward the center of Earth. His dad always said that physics was everywhere.

But Dev didn't want to think about physics. He wanted to think about Mount McKinley, then wolves and caribou. After all, he wasn't at science camp.

"You guys might want to rest," Javier suggested. "We'll be in the plane for a while."

"I'll keep track of our progress," Dev said to the rest of the team, glancing at the GPS in his lap.

"I'll stay up with you," Russell offered.

"Then we'll take the second shift," Sage said as she wadded a jacket into a makeshift pillow and leaned her head against the window. Mari nodded and did the same. Dev noticed that she looked a little sick.

After climbing steadily for a while, the plane leveled off. They flew through wispy clouds. "Cloud cover is always worse in the summer," the pilot announced from the front seat. "Lots of folks come to Alaska and don't even get to see Denali."

"Denali is a native name for Mount McKinley?" Dev asked.

"Yes," the pilot replied. "It translates to 'The High One.'"

At that moment, the clouds seemed to part dramatically, and they could see that the High One was truly high.

MCKINLEY OR DENALI?

The highest mountain in Alaska has had many names in many different languages. Since 1896, it has been called Mount McKinley, after President McKinley. However, the president never actually set foot in Alaska. For this reason, many believe the state's most impressive peak should be officially retitled using one of the names chosen by the native people. Denali means "The High One" in Athabaskan. Denali is also the name of the national state park where the peak is located.

Mount McKinley is 20,237 feet (6,168 meters) high, and temperatures on the summit can get as low as minus 95 degrees Fahrenheit (minus 60 degrees Celsius). The snow on the top half of the mountain never melts. This mountain is part of the 600-mile Alaska Range, which is over sixty-five million years old.

Geologically speaking, it is not a volcano. It is a mass of magma, or underground lava, that cooled under the Earth's surface long ago. Over millions of years, the tectonic plates below have moved and pushed the mass upward. It is still growing—about one millimeter each year.

CHAPTER 6

A HIGH POINT

"**W**hoa, it's huge," Russell said, leaning forward to gaze out. The view of the mountain filled the airplane window. The colors were so deep, they hardly appeared real: the dense green of the forest at the base; the varied grays of the lower ridges, shadowed with midnight blue; and the glimmering whites of the wind-battered ice and snow on the jagged peaks.

Dev forced himself to look away so he could check the GPS and the map. "Is this the South

Summit?" he asked. "Because we need the highest peak."

Russell grabbed a corner of the map so they could both see it. Dev pointed to their location. "The North Summit is the second highest point. I don't want to get the wrong one."

"This here's the south," said the pilot.

Dev trusted the pilot, and he also trusted the GPS. He took a picture and sent it to Bull Gordon. In less than a minute, the ancam buzzed, but the message gave Dev little relief. Even though the photo had been accepted, they still needed two more shots to earn the next clue.

Now they were flying directly over the mountain. Just looking at the layers of ice and snow gave Dev shivers. He wasn't a big fan of cold weather, or heights.

"Maybe we should wake Sage and Mari, so they can see this," Russell wondered out loud, but they decided against it. They didn't know how late they'd have to be up that night, and rest was the key to endurance. Dev guessed they still had a long way to go on this leg of the race. The Arctic was a big place, and they weren't even technically there yet.

When the girls woke up, the plane was leaving the mountains behind. The ground was leveling out into a gently rolling grassland.

"Did we get the shot of the summit?" Sage asked, all business, even though she was still rubbing her eyes.

"Yeah," Dev answered. "I took some other

shots, too, just so you guys could see." He handed the ancam to Mari, who was sitting behind him.

"These are amazing," Mari said as she scrolled through. "I can't believe we slept so long, and that it's still so light out."

"It's good that it's light," Sage said. "Now that we're flying over the tundra, we should be able to finish the clue."

In the tundra, the intensely cold winter meant that much of the ground beneath the surface stayed frozen the whole year. In some places, only a foot of topsoil would thaw enough to support summer plant life. Small shrubs, wildflowers, and plants like moss had adapted to grow in these tricky conditions.

Dev and Russell took their turn to rest. When they awoke, the terrain looked much the same.

The pilot was flying lower, so they could spy wild-life below.

"We've seen lots of birds," Mari told them. "They migrate here because of all the summer food."

"What food?" Russell asked, peering out the window.

"Bugs, for one," Mari said. "Something has to eat all those mosquitos."

Dev absentmindedly scratched a bite on his neck.

"We also spotted an Arctic fox," Mari said. "It was hard to see. Its summer coat really blends in."

Dev thought it was amazing how many of the animals changed from season to season. Thick, fluffy, and pure white in the winter, the Arctic fox's coat was the warmest of any animal. Every spring, the fox shed the long fur and its coat turned brown or gray for camouflage.

"But we haven't seen wolves or caribou—or reindeer," added Sage. "Whatever we're looking for."

"Reindeer and caribou are the same kind of deer," Mari clarified.

"Well, we haven't seen any," Sage insisted.

"Uh, what's that?" Russell asked, his binoculars pointed straight ahead.

Dev focused his own binoculars. It looked as if the land were moving in a giant brown wave.

"Nice work, Russell," Sage said, but it wasn't as if they could have missed it. As the plane flew closer, they could see that the herd of caribou before them was hundreds, maybe thousands, strong. They moved together, in one fluid motion.

"Caribou sometimes migrate over fifty miles a day," said Mari as she watched the herd run.

"That's nothing compared to Santa's reindeer," Russell said.

Dev thought it was pretty funny, but neither of the girls laughed. Both of their binoculars were focused on a nearby crest.

"Wolves," Sage whispered. "Gray wolves."

Instead of sounding excited to have closed in on the two answers to their clue, Sage's voice was filled with dread.

Mari looked out the other window and lowered her binoculars. "They're on the other side, too. They're looking for stragglers, for the young or weak. They'll target one and separate it from the pack. Caribou are faster than wolves, but they can't outrun a pack. Wolves are just too clever."

Feeling stunned, Dev took a picture of the caribou as quickly as possible. "Would you please
turn toward that ridge?" he called over the cock-
pit partition.

"Sure thing," replied the pilot.

Dev was able to focus in for a closeup of one of
the wolves. With its ears pricked forward, it
appeared to be good-natured, even frisky, but
Dev knew that expression could change quickly.

"Did you get the shots?" Sage asked. "Let's wait for the approval and then move on."

Dev was used to Sage prompting him, but she sounded particularly urgent. "Okay," Dev answered. When he looked out the window again, he saw a young deer lagging behind the herd, by just a few steps at first. But he felt like he knew what would happen next. He was relieved to be distracted by the ancam's familiar buzz.

CREATURE FEATURE

CARIBOU

SCIENTIFIC NAME: *Rangifer tarandus*

TYPE: mammal

RANGE: spread across northern sections of North America, from Idaho and Washington into Canada and Alaska; northern Europe, in Norway and Finland; Russia

FOOD: mosses; lichens; grasses; ferns; leaves of certain shrubs and trees, especially willow

Every year, the caribou herds of North America undertake one of the longest migrations of any land-dwelling animal. In the summer, they find ample food, few predators, and relief from pesky insects near the coast of the Arctic Ocean. In the winter, the herd waits out the coldest part of the season farther inland in the forest. But most of the caribou's year is spent trekking back and forth across the tundra.

Caribou's bodies are made for enduring the cold. Their hooves have four toes that spread out wide and act like snowshoes so they don't sink into the snow and soft ice. They also have two layers of fur. The one on the outside is made of guard hairs that trap heat underneath. Their strong sense of smell is a bonus, too. They can sniff out lichen and other plants hidden in up to five feet of snow.

CHAPTER 7

STRAIGHT INTO THE CIRCLE

The members of Team Red were glad to be done with the three-part clue, but they were absolutely thrilled to get off the pontoon plane.

"My knees are stuck," Russell said, shaking out his legs.

"Don't worry. You don't have far to walk," Javier said as he stepped onto the floating dock. "You just need to get to that boat." The team looked to where their chaperone had pointed.

"And you may want to hurry. Dev, you'll find a replacement backpack in your cabin."

Dev still wore his quicksand-caked shirt, and by now, the hardened mud was like a crunchy second skin. It'd feel good to clean up.

The boat looked like a mini cruise ship. As he marched up the gangplank, Dev realized that there were at least two other teams already on board. He had expected that one team would be ahead of them, but now they had dropped to third place—or worse.

"Slipped a spot, didn't you?" Dev heard the de facto leader of Team Purple say to Sage as they shuffled past.

"The race isn't over, Eliza," Sage replied in a flat tone. The other girl was wearing a cozy lavender fleece that didn't match her frosty stare.

"Hi, Eliza," Mari offered cheerily, but no one else spoke.

"Dude, you made it!" called a kid in a lime-green jacket. He was talking to Russell, who had known all of Team Green before the race.

"Yeah, we're not out yet," Russell replied with a shrug. He was so good-natured. Dev watched as Russell fist-bumped the two guys on deck without losing step with the rest of Team Red.

Dev had always thought it was odd that Russell had ended up on the red team, when his friends from home were together on Team Green. There was more to that story, Dev was sure. But ever since the first day, Russell had seemed committed to Team Red. Dev was happy to have

Russell with them. He was "good stock," as his grandmother would say.

Three other teams climbed aboard the boat before it departed. Later that night, at dinner, one of the organizers announced that the teams would set off the next morning in the same order that they had arrived on the ship.

"So we're stuck in third place," Sage said.

"We're in the top half," Russell suggested optimistically. "We'll catch up."

The six teams sat at separate tables. All conversations were hushed. After checking the GPS, Dev was certain they were heading north. At the speed they were traveling, they would be near the Arctic Circle by morning and there would still be two teams ahead of them.

Dev was quiet. He had been revisiting all of his decisions from earlier in the day. Could he have foreseen the quicksand and plotted a different path across the river? Should they have trailblazed down the mountain, despite the threat of rockslides? Had there been a quicker route over Denali and across the tundra?

"What are you thinking about?" Mari asked.

Dev glanced up, caught off guard. "Uh, I just remembered this funny dream I had," Dev said. "At first it seems like it is all about *The Wild Life*, but then my dad shows up out of nowhere." He was surprised when his teammates seemed interested. He went on to give them some of the details, including the plaid Bermuda shorts. "It seemed so real."

Sage and Russell muffled laughs, but Mari looked thoughtful. "Maybe it means something," she suggested, picking at the crust of her vegetable potpie with a fork. "My mom always tries to interpret her dreams."

Mari's words were with Dev as he fell asleep in his cabin that night, and they were the first thing he remembered in the morning—because he'd had the exact same dream again.

But his mind was soon clear of all other thoughts. A new clue had arrived via the ancam. Dev grabbed Russell and they rushed to the girls' cabin.

```
Fatty warmth
Hollow hairs
Paddle paws
```

Black skin

Soaking in sun.

Power predator

Stalking sea ice

And everything

Underneath.

"It's a polar bear!" Mari exclaimed. She took a deep breath and her eyes sparkled like she had just received a present. "The fatty warmth is the thick layer of fat that insulates them from the cold water. But on land, they rely on their heavy coat, which has hollow hairs, like caribou and Arctic foxes, to hold their body heat. Their paws are wide like paddles for swimming, and their black skin is an adaptation for warmth. Black absorbs more heat from the sun." Mari let out a sigh. Dev thought she was done, but then she took another quick breath. "Obviously they are powerful predators, especially on the sea ice. They wait at a hole for a seal or a whale to come up to breathe. All it takes is a swipe of their mighty paw, and it's the end of the prey and the start of dinner."

Mari's three teammates hesitated, wondering if she had more to say.

"Polar bears are one of my favorites," she admitted, blushing.

"Well then, let's go find one," said Russell.

CREATURE FEATURE

POLAR BEAR

SCIENTIFIC NAME: *Ursus maritimus*

TYPE: mammal

RANGE: Arctic regions

FOOD: seals, seal pups, walruses, beached whales, grass, seaweed

Scientists believe that polar bears descended from brown bears, but the polar bear has adapted to life in the Arctic. While other northern bears hibernate, most polar bears are active in the winter. In fact, it is a prime time for hunting.

With furry paws to keep them from slipping, they prowl the ice, smelling out seal dens and waiting by breathing holes. But when most of the sea ice melts in summer, the polar bear no longer has an advantage. Despite being good swimmers, they cannot catch seals or walruses in open water. Instead, late summer often finds polar bears on the mainland, waiting for a big freeze.

Pregnant mothers are an exception. They do hibernate, digging an ice den where they have their cubs in the winter months. By early spring, plump from mom's milk, the cubs will be ready to brave the chilly Arctic world.

CHAPTER 8

A COINCIDENCE?

From the deck of the boat, the red team could see the coast on one side and the vast expanse of the Arctic Ocean on the other. There was a rustic port on the shore, but Dev stared out at the ocean. Dev had never seen anything like it. Nearby, a single slab of sea ice floated, but the rest of the view was a rich, watery blue.

"Good to see you guys are up and at 'em." Dev flinched when Javier spoke. He hadn't expected their chaperone to join them just yet. "Cool, huh?"

"It's definitely cool," Dev replied, "but the question is, is it cold?"

"What do you mean?" Russell asked with a shiver. "It's the Arctic. It's freezing! And it's summer!"

Dev hesitated. Maybe he shouldn't get into it, but his teammates seemed to be waiting to hear what he had to say. "I read this article about how the oceans are getting warmer. So, even though the Arctic is still cold, not as much sea ice is forming in the winter, and it isn't lasting as long into the summer months."

"But sea ice gives seals, polar bears, and walruses a safe place to rest," Mari said with concern.

"That's not all it does," Dev said. He paused again, feeling unsure. "It takes physics to explain it." Then he launched into the full explanation.

"Because the ice is white, it reflects sunlight back toward space. But the dark blue ocean absorbs sunlight. And the light's energy warms up the ocean. It becomes a whole cycle: The less white sea ice there is, the more light energy the dark water absorbs. The more light energy it absorbs, the warmer it gets, and the more it melts the sea ice! So, the sea ice works like a kind of air conditioner . . . for the whole planet."

When Dev looked back at his teammates, he was certain they were seeing him in a different way. Great. He'd really done it now. His whole goal for the summer—his goal for the race—was to be normal, to be someone other than the nerdy science kid.

Dev looked at the lonely slab of sea ice and wished he could be on it.

"I see one!" Mari yelled out suddenly. "A polar bear!" She pointed frantically toward the coastline. Dev, knowing it was his responsibility, rushed over and took a shot before any of the other teams could react. Then he remembered it didn't matter. The teams were leaving the boat in the same order they had arrived.

The polar bear was gigantic. It wasn't hard to believe that it was the largest species of bear in the world. Mari leaned over the boat's railing.

"You're not at the zoo," Sage reminded her.

"Well," Mari said, "until the ice forms again, he's stuck here with people watching him all the time."

At that moment, a host of organizers rushed onto the deck, ushering Team Purple down the gangplank.

As soon as they were gone, Javier pulled his team aside. "The green team will leave in ten minutes, and then you. Go downstairs and put on your warmest gear. Be back here in fifteen minutes."

Dev thought it was funny how the chaperones had to be secretive. Javier obviously knew what they were doing, but he wouldn't tell them. So, a few minutes later, when the team followed the organizers down the gangplank and into a hidden cove, they were amazed by what happened next.

"The helicopter will take you to a glacier, where you will drive dogsleds to the final checkpoint." All four team members stared at Javier. "Come on, let's go!"

Javier helped them in, one by one, and then climbed in next to them. He swung the door shut, and the helicopter lifted into the sky.

"We're going to a glacier?" Sage asked.

"Yes. And you're going to dogsled," Javier answered, barely containing his own excitement. "You will each get a team of dogs and a sled. I get to follow behind."

"Dev, it's just like in your dream!" Mari declared.

Dev had thought about that. It was eerily similar.

The helicopter ride was short. As they approached an imposing mountain, Dev could see two rocky cliffs with a smooth, sloping, snow-covered surface making a wide pathway in between. "That's the glacier," Javier said. "It's perfect terrain for dogsledding."

The landing skids had barely set down on the ice when Javier whipped open the door. "The dog

teams are over there," he said. "Go pick your-
selves some winners."

"We need to get some big, strong dogs," Russell
announced as they set off for where the dogs
were tied in groups of four. "We've got catching
up to do."

"These guys look good," Sage said, looking at
some sweet-eyed malamutes with broad shoulders
and thick coats. "Maybe we should go with them."

Mari nodded. Dev was about to agree when he
saw another group of dogs on the far end. "Wait,"
he directed, walking down the line. He realized
that each row had four sets of four dogs each, so
he assumed they picked one row and each team
member would get one of the sets.

When he came to the last row, he knelt
down. One dog stepped toward him. She was a

caramel-frosted husky with wise eyes. The dog looked familiar. That's when Dev realized it was the lead dog from his dream. He placed his hand on her head, and she returned his unblinking stare. "You guys," he called. "What about this row?"

Mari immediately strode toward him, but the others hung back for a moment.

"They look good to me," Mari said.

"Aren't they kind of small?" Russell pointed out.

"No," Dev replied with a shrug. "There's four pulling each sled. And those are the sleds over there. They're not that big. It's not like we packed a lot of baggage." Dev was trying to sound rational, but he couldn't really explain it. He just *had* to have that dog on his team. It was some kind of sign. He knew it. He didn't need a scientific theorem to tell him that it was meant to be.

He knelt down again and buried his hands in the thick fur around the dog's neck. His fingers touched something. A collar. He quickly searched and found what he was looking for. It was smooth and round. It was a name tag, and it read TUCKER. A chill jolted through every nerve in Dev's body. It was the name from his dream!

SLOW-MOVING GLACIERS

A glacier is the buildup of snow. Glaciers only form in extremely cold places over long periods of time. These places are: near the North Pole, near the South Pole, and high in the mountains.

Over the years, as more and more snow piles up, the newer snow pushes down on the older snow, and the snow near the bottom turns to ice. This process goes on for hundreds, thousands, and, in some cases, millions of years.

After a long time, all the frozen ice becomes

very heavy. This weight causes the glacier to slide, very slowly, downhill. The world's fastest glacier is in Greenland. It moves over ten miles a year. On average, most glaciers only move about one hundred feet per year.

CHAPTER 9
SHORT CUT, LONG FALL

"**W**e have to make a choice, and we're going with these," Dev declared. One of the race organizers heard him and rushed over, directing other workers to bring the sleds.

Sage and Russell exchanged glances but quickly gave in. After all, they were in the middle of a race. They needed to hurry.

"We'll hitch them up," a worker said. "You should grab any of the extra equipment you want."

Dev hurried over to a display, thinking they might have some cool gadgets, but everything was low-tech. He picked up some rope, an ice pick, and a bag of dog treats, and rushed back to where the dogs were being attached to the sleds. One of the workers gave them a quick lesson on how to drive the team, and then it was time to go.

As Dev was stepping onto the sled footboards, an attendant unexpectedly put his hand on Dev's shoulder. "You made a good choice with this team," he said in a kind voice. "These huskies are smart *and* fast."

Dev was relieved to hear him say that. He was even more relieved to see that a map had appeared on the ancam. The end point was marked with a red pin. It seemed like an easy trip, and Dev was determined to find the quickest route possible. He looked over his shoulder at the rest of the team. "Ready?" he called. Everyone was in place. He turned back around and yelled, "Hike!"

In the lead position on the front right, Tucker leapt forward. The rest of the dogs followed.

Driving a dogsled over an ancient Alaskan glacier felt way more natural than Dev would have thought possible. It was straight out of his dream. With the cold, crisp air in his lungs and the vast blue horizon before him, Dev started to think about how he had dismissed things like dreams all his life. He'd based everything on science. Maybe he should trust his instincts more.

His dream had led him to Tucker, and she seemed like the most reliable sled dog ever.

He knew that Mari, Sage, and Russell were behind him, but in some ways he felt like he and his dog team were all alone. Then, after a while, Dev noticed dark shadows on the horizon. It was another team, and the red team was gaining on them!

Dev was consumed with the chase. It only took a few minutes to overtake the other sleds. As they got closer, he could tell it was Team Purple. It looked like a sled had capsized. Because no one was hurt, Dev kept moving. When he looked over his shoulder, the red team sleds were right on his tail. Dev kept going, finding an easy rhythm on the packed snow. He noticed a bird—a bald eagle—high above, effortlessly soaring in the sky.

Dev checked the ancam again. It looked like they were approaching a fork in the road. A shortcut! He signaled to the team that he was going to stop. "Whoa," he called, and waited for the others to pull up next to him.

"It looks like this is a shorter path," he said, pointing on the map.

"Really?" Sage asked. The V in Sage's brow was back, digging its way between her eyes.

"It'd be faster," Dev said. This would be the perfect way to make up for the time he had cost them the day before.

"It looks like Team Green stayed on the main pass," Russell pointed out. "These runner tracks are fresh."

The eagle circled directly over the shortcut route. It had to be a sign.

"We should take the shortcut. Trust me." Dev stepped back onto the footboards and yelled, "Hike!" Tucker and his team took off, and the others followed.

Dev liked the fact that they'd chosen their own path. But he soon noticed that the sled did not feel as steady as it had before. The runners made crunching sounds on the snow, instead of clean slices on the main track. Something didn't seem right. They weren't moving as fast on this path. At their current rate, the shortcut would take just as long—or longer—than the other option.

He didn't want to admit he was wrong, yet he couldn't waste any more of the team's time. He waved to his teammates, but just as he called to his dogs to pull up, he heard a yelp. The sled slammed to a stop. Something was wrong. Very wrong. It took Dev a moment to realize that the other front dog, Tucker's partner, had disappeared.

"Help!" Dev called, racing forward on the crusty snow. He did not get very far. Just ahead of the sled, the ground had opened up. Dev crawled on hands and knees to look over the edge of the ice. There, dangling from his harness, was the

gray-and-white husky. When the dog saw him, he whimpered.

Soon Javier and Sage were by his side. Mari and Russell stayed with the other dogs.

"It's a crevasse," Javier said.

"A crack in the glacier," Dev noted.

"Uh-huh," Javier agreed. "One glacier must have slipped or shifted over another. It can force a chasm." The word sounded empty and bleak.

"What about the dog?" Sage asked.

"I'm figuring that out," Dev answered. "It's my fault, and I *will* figure it out."

CREATURE FEATURE

BALD EAGLE

SCIENTIFIC NAME: *Haliaeetus leucocephalus*

TYPE: bird

RANGE: Canada and USA, especially northern regions; Mexico

FOOD: fish; small mammals; carrion (dead meat)

It's not bald! With stark white feathers on its head and neck, this powerful bird can appear bald from afar, but the layered pattern of those feathers provides warmth in the Arctic chill. The feathers are made of keratin, the same material in the eagle's beak and talons—and human fingernails.

Bald eagles are masters of flight, using special wind currents called thermals to soar. Because soaring does not require them to flap their wings, it saves energy, which they can use to make deep dives toward the water to catch fish with their sharp talons.

While they are talented at fishing, bald eagles also have a habit of eating carrion or stealing fresh kills from other animals. For this reason, Ben Franklin once argued against the bald eagle being the national bird.

CHAPTER 10

ARCTIC BLAST

Dev was talking under his breath, mumbling, because his mind was working on the problem at hand. He had read about some early science expeditions in the Arctic and Antarctic. When dogs had been sick or injured, the explorers had to shoot them. Dev couldn't imagine anything worse.

"See his front leg?" Dev asked, pointing. "It's about to slip from the harness. We can't just pull him up by the tug line, or he might fall out completely."

Still leaning over the edge, he gave Sage orders: First, to get the rope and ice pick from his sled. Second, to go to Tucker and reassure the lead dog.

Tucker was standing strong, but she was working hard to support the fallen dog—and not slip into the crevasse herself.

Dev worked quickly, tying the rope into something like a lasso. Javier held his legs as he leaned forward and tried to loop the rope around the dog.

"Got it," Dev yelled. "Now, Javier, pull him up with the ice pick. Use it like a lever."

Javier hooked the ice pick through the rope and tugged with both hands until the dog was beside them on the solid ice.

"That's awesome," Sage cried. "You saved him."

Dev wrapped his arms around the dog and buried his face in his fur. He listened as Javier directed Sage and the others to turn around. The chaperone insisted they backtrack and return to the main route.

Sage hesitated. "I don't think we should split up," she said.

"It'll be fine," Javier assured her. "Just get as much of the team to the finish line as possible. We'll be there soon."

As soon as Sage started shepherding the others in their retreat, Javier turned to Dev.

"I was about to tell them to turn around," Dev said. "If I had just stopped ten seconds sooner."

"Races prompt hasty decisions," Javier said, sweeping his hands over the husky. "That's their nature. But the quick thinking you did here was far more essential. You have an engineer's mind, and it saved this dog." Dev took in those words. They would make his dad proud. "I'm pretty sure the dog is fine," Javier continued, "but he'll ride on my sled, just in case. You'll be good with three dogs, I think. Let's stay together until we're back on the main route, then you can go ahead." Dev stared at Javier. "You're the one that's in a race, after all."

Dev's mind was still on his mistake. He had to shake that. He turned back to his three remaining huskies and spoke to them softly as he checked their harnesses and adjusted the tug lines. They lifted their chins toward him and wagged their tails. Dogs were such exceptional animals, and he wanted to earn their trust, to be part of their team.

After an extra pat for Tucker, they were off again. Dev followed Javier's sled, and they were soon back to the main path.

"Go ahead!" Javier called with a wave. Almost instantly, Tucker and the other two dogs began to lengthen their stride.

The dogs could follow the path left by the other teams. Dev just wanted to make it to the finish. Each team member had to complete the challenge, or the team would not move on to the next leg.

That's what Dev was thinking about as the dogs pulled him to the crest of a slope. From there, Dev could see another team, a set of four sleds, in front of him. Team Yellow. Just beyond their leader there was a Wild Life banner, flapping in the brisk wind.

At first, Dev was crushed. He could never catch that team's leader before the finish line . . . but he could pass their fourth sled.

All Team Red needed to place ahead of Team Yellow was for Dev to beat one of their members over the finish line.

"Hike!" he yelled, and the dogs responded.

No part of Dev's dream made sense to him anymore. The only thing he was sure of was that Tucker was a top-rate lead dog. Her tongue flapped as she picked up the pace. The team was gaining on the group of sleds, but the banner was getting closer, too. Dev leaned forward, willing his dogs to run their best. As they neared the other sled, Dev called, "On by!" He wasn't certain it was the right command, but Tucker and the others surged ahead of the last yellow sled just before they crossed the finish line.

Mari and Sage were cheering as they stormed Dev. Spent, Dev staggered off the footboards and tumbled to the ground right next to Tucker. Tucker, who had been all business during the race, licked Dev's face. Dev squeezed his eyes shut as the warm tongue swiped his cheeks and nose.

"It's nice of you to join us."

Dev's eyes shot back open at the sound of Bull Gordon's booming voice. He sat up. "Yes, sir."

"No need to get up," said the spokesman of *The Wild Life*. "You've had a long couple of days."

"Well, we're in Alaska in the middle of the summer, sir," Dev replied. "All the days are long."

A smile slowly stretched across Bull's tan face.

"You make a good point, son. And your team put in another good effort—not as good as some, but we won't have a winner until we've run the whole race." Bull reached down, wrapped his fist around Dev's wrist, and pulled him up. Tucker switched to licking Dev's hand. "You were the fourth team to arrive," Bull Gordon continued, "but another team broke the Wild Life rules. They were disqualified, so Team Red is now in third place. Maybe you can take advantage of the other team's misfortune."

"Yes, sir," Dev replied, but he didn't mean it. He didn't want to win that way. He wanted to win on his own merits. He looked around at his teammates. He was certain they all wanted the same thing. If this leg of the race had taught him anything, it was that he needed to trust his instincts, even when they were based in scientific fact.

Bull Gordon touched his hand to the brim of his hat. "Good day, Team Red," he said before striding away.

Dev waited until the spokesman was out of earshot. "Disqualified?" he asked his team. "What's that about?"

"We don't know," Sage told him. "It was Team Orange. The organizers already picked them up by helicopter and took them back to the boat."

At that moment, Bull Gordon opened the door to the temporary tent. Dev peeked inside and saw members of Teams Yellow, Purple, and Green drinking hot chocolate. The scene looked much more lighthearted than he felt. With only one leg left and a team disqualified, things felt very serious. He rubbed Tucker's ears as he looked at his teammates. They had one more chance, and each of them would have to give their all if they wanted to be winners of *The Wild Life*.

Want to know what happens when *The Wild Life* moves to the African savanna? Read on for a glimpse of the next race course in

If there was a chance to answer a clue while on the bus, Team Red needed to seize it. They were currently in third place, so they had a lot of catching up to do. All five of the remaining teams were on the bus, crammed in with tourists who were anxious to start their safaris. The teams were anxious, too.

"I can't believe the orange team was booted, just for sending in the wrong photo," Russell said under his breath so only members of Team Red could hear.

"Julia from Team Purple told me they doctored the photo," Sage added. "That's why they were kicked out of the race." Her gaze darted between her teammates and passing stretches of dry, grassy land.

"I don't get how they could do that," Dev stated, pulling out the team ancam. The ancam was the team's soul communication device, and Dev was in charge of it. "As far as I can tell, the system is locked. There is no way to alter the photos you take, or to load different files. It would take an expert hack."

Mari tried to hide her smile. Dev was as much of a nerd about tech and physics as she was about animals. That was his thing. If he couldn't figure out how to tamper with the ancam and their answers, Mari doubted anyone could.

"Do you really think Bull Gordon would kick out a team just for giving a wrong answer?" Russell wondered. "Seems extreme." Bull Gordon was the head of *The Wild Life*. Before he had become the spokesperson for the race, he had been a wilderness explorer and adventurer.

"It seems unlikely. And unfair," Sage admitted. "But we're down to the wire. Maybe it's his way of letting everyone know it's serious. There's no room for mistakes if you're going to win."

Russell sighed so loudly that the whole team turned to him. He looked up, suddenly aware. "I wonder what he'd do if he found out someone really cheated."

"They'd be gone in an instant," Sage replied. "And they'd deserve it."

Mari looked at Sage. The team leader had become much more of a team player since the start of the race, but Mari suspected that Sage's old grit—her we're-in-it-to-win-it attitude—had returned.

"Well, we won't submit any bad photos," Dev reassured everyone, "just as long as Mari points me in the right direction."

"What?" Mari felt her face grow hot, and not from the burn of the sun.

"What do you mean 'what?' You are the wiz when it comes to these clues."

"But we're a team," Mari insisted.

"Yes," Sage agreed. "And we're lucky to have you. You could have easily ended up with the other Smarties on Team Purple."

Mari lowered her head again and stared at a rusty spot on the bus floor. She pressed harder on her wrist. Her brain ached. It was all too much.

*   *   *

"Good to see you all made it." Bull Gordon greeted them from below, waving up to the contestants on the bus. The battered rim of his trademark fedora shielded his face from the sun, but his smile was still gleaming and bright.

Mari and the rest of the red team were already striding up the aisle toward the stairs. They wanted to be the first off the double-decker. Mari couldn't wait to be back on solid ground.

"Excuse us," one of the girls from Team Purple said, forcing her way into the aisle, right in front of Mari.

"They should let us go first, anyway, since we're ahead of them," Eliza, the Team Purple leader insisted. "Remember, the red team is back in third place."

Mari's eyes narrowed. She was somewhat insulted that Sage had said she would fit in with the purple team. Sure, all the members were smart, but that was about it.

Mari sighed and stepped back, letting the purple-clad contestants leave their seats.

"Hey. Us, too," a boy in lime green cut in with a chuckle. His team had been in the seats on the opposite side of the aisle. "'Cause we're in the lead."

Mari glanced over her shoulder. Sage nodded. It was Russell who tried not to roll his eyes. There was history there. Russell had known all the guys on Team Green from before the race. Mari remembered that they'd played football together, or something like that. It was weird, how Russell had ended up on Team Red instead of Team Green.

The four boys strutted off, each with his own swagger.

"There go your bros," Dev whispered.

"Yeah, right," Russell whispered back.

Sage nudged Mari's elbow, and Mari followed the leaders.

"One map per team," Bull Gordon said as he placed a folded brochure in Mari's hand.

Mari gave him a quick smile. To her, Bull Gordon seemed like a super cool uncle or a fun science teacher.

She looked around the small rest stop, drew in a deep breath, and started feeling more like herself again.

"Two team members come with me," Bull announced. "Two stay and study the map."

Mari held up the map, and Russell moved next

to her. Sage and Dev headed off with the other group. Both Mari and Russell watched as the others walked away.

"Can you imagine being kicked out by Bull Gordon?" she said. "That would be the worst. Especially if you didn't cheat."

"It'd be worse if you did cheat," Russell replied. "'Cause then he'd be all like, 'I'm disappointed in you. That's not how we run this race.'" Russell shook his head. "Nothing would be worse than that." Russell was staring out at the rolling land, but he wasn't really looking at it. He turned to Mari. "You know? There's a team that did cheat. For real. And they're still in the race."

Mari didn't have a response.

"I didn't tell anyone. It didn't feel right." Russell's face was blank for a long time. Then he shifted the weight of his hiking pack and focused in on the map. "So, where are we?" he asked, glancing around for landmarks while Mari did the unfolding.

"We're right here," Mari declared, relieved by the change of subject. There was a red star in the middle of the map, right next to a tourist rest stop. "We're in the middle of the Serengeti."

"That's, like, famous. Right?"

"Right. We're going to see giant herds of grazing animals. And predators. Lots of predators. It'll be amazing." Already, the possibilities churned through Mari's head. The Serengeti was the perfect place for the last leg of the race. Here, they would witness wild animals being truly wild, out on the open plains. It would be a real safari.

Mari had once read that the word "safari" came from the Swahili word that means "journey." The last leg of their journey was about to begin. Mari looked up to see Sage and Dev rushing back. "We've got our clue!" Dev yelled. He held out the ancam, and they all crowded around to read.

```
This earth pig
Can really dig.
It hears its foes,
And smells its food.
Its tongue is covered
With something like glue.
```

READ *SAVANNA SHOWDOWN* TO FIND OUT WHAT HAPPENS NEXT!

I SURVIVED

Find out how a kid could survive the greatest disasters in history!

Read the bestselling series by Lauren Tarshis!

Available in print and eBook editions

Test your survival skills at **scholastic. com/isurvived**

■SCHOLASTIC

ISURVIVEDe

WHEN DISASTER STRIKES, THE ONLY THING YOU CAN COUNT ON IS YOURSELF!

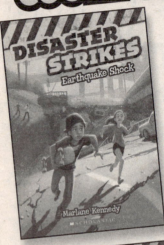

Earthquakes in California. Tornados in Oklahoma.
Blizzards in Michigan. Volcanoes in Alaska. Find out what these
kids do to launch into survival mode on disaster day.

The Rescue Princesses

These are no ordinary princesses—
they're Rescue Princesses!